MARY-KATE AND A

IN ACTI

Makeup Shake-Up

A novelization by Eliza Willard
based on the teleplay
by Robin Riordan

📕HarperEntertainment
An Imprint of HarperCollins*Publishers*

A PARACHUTE PRESS BOOK

A PARACHUTE PRESS BOOK

Parachute Publishing, L.L.C.
156 Fifth Avenue, Suite 302
New York, NY 10010

Published by
HarperEntertainment
An Imprint of HarperCollins*Publishers*
10 East 53rd Street, New York, NY 10022-5299

ISBN 0-06-009302-1

HarperCollins®, ****®, and HarperEntertainment™ are trademarks of HarperCollins Publishers Inc.

First printing: October 2002

Printed in China

Visit the on-line book boutique on the World Wide Web at
www.mary-kateandashley.com.

Visit HarperEntertainment on the World Wide Web at
www.harpercollins.com

10 9 8 7 6 5 4 3 2 1

CHAPTER ONE
A New Assignment

"Digital diary. Two fifty-five P.M. New York City," Ashley's sister, Mary-Kate, whispered into her bracelet. "We are at a fashion show on our latest assignment."

Ashley giggled. Mary-Kate loved using special-agent equipment—especially her high-tech wrist computer. Sometimes Ashley wondered if her sister became a special agent for all the cool gadgets.

But the two of them joined Headquarters, a top-secret organization, for one reason: to fight super-villains and save the world!

Ashley stood onstage behind a heavy red curtain. She pushed the curtain aside and peeked at the audience. She glanced right and left, searching for signs of trouble.

Mary-Kate flipped her bracelet closed. "See anything suspicious, Special Agent Amber?" Mary-Kate asked.

Amber was Ashley's code name.

"Not yet, Special Agent Misty," Ashley replied, using Mary-Kate's code name. "But we must be missing something. Headquarters wouldn't send us here without a good reason."

"Let's find that model, Dominique, before the show starts," their friend, Rodney Choy said. "Headquarters told us to stick close to her, remember?"

Rod worked with Mary-Kate and Ashley. He drove the girls wherever they needed to go.

"Right," Mary-Kate agreed. "Let's move."

Their puppy, Quincy, scampered ahead. He was a beige Scottie. But Quincy wasn't an ordinary dog. He wasn't even a *real* dog. He was a talking robot—a very smart one! He helped Mary-Kate and Ashley with all of their cases.

Ashley, Mary-Kate, Rodney, and Quincy waded through the crowded backstage area toward the dressing rooms. Ashley removed a computer printout from her pocketbook.

"Did you know that over eight million people live in New York City?" Ashley asked. Her eyes scanned the printout. "And that an estimated forty million visited here last year?"

"Really? That's cool," Mary-Kate told her. "But look around. You don't need a fact sheet to tell you that this town is packed with people."

"Yeah," Rod agreed. "How are we supposed to figure out where Dominique is?"

Quincy stopped and sniffed the air. "Girls, she's in there," he whispered.

"Thanks, Quincy." Ashley patted him on the head.

Quincy's radar sniffer could find just about anyone!

Mary-Kate knocked on the dressing-room door.

"Come in!" a voice called from the other side.

They entered the room. A tall girl with short red hair stood to greet them. "You must be Misty and Amber," she said. "I'm Dominique."

"Nice to meet you," Mary-Kate answered.

"This is our friend, Rod."

"I'm glad you're here," Dominique said. "Something weird is going on. The other models have been acting very strange lately."

"Strange?" Ashley asked. "What do you mean?"

Before Dominique could answer, a woman burst into the dressing room.

"Dominique!" the woman called. She was carrying a large pink basket filled with cosmetics. Her blond hair was pulled into two big, puffy pigtails. She set the basket on Dominique's dressing table.

"My name is Sylvie," the woman introduced herself. Ashley noticed that she had a French accent.

"I am a cosmetics artist for Madame La Rouge," Sylvie said. "This basket is a gift from her."

"Wow! You work for Renee La Rouge?" Mary-Kate asked. "I've heard of her. She owns Blush Cosmetics in Paris."

Dominique glanced at the basket and frowned. "Madame La Rouge has been sending me these baskets for months, Sylvie. It's very nice of her, but please tell her that I don't need any more cosmetics."

"Nonsense." Sylvie took a round cosmetics case from the basket and opened it. It had a mirror on one side and powder on the other.

"This is Face Values, Madame La Rouge's new line of cosmetics," she explained. "Madame would like you and all of the top models to appear in the Face Values commercials. Won't you at least try it?"

"Well, I guess it couldn't hurt," Dominique said.

Sylvie powdered Dominique's face.

Dominique studied the bright red powder case. "It's nice," she said. "But I don't wear a lot of cosmetics. I'm more into the natural look."

"We are, too," Mary-Kate and Ashley agreed.

Sylvie frowned. "I'm sure Face Values will change your mind." She pulled a jar from the basket. "Let's try this foot cream next." She rubbed some on Dominique's feet.

Dominique searched through the basket.

She pulled out a small tube and read the label. "'Do As I Say Lip Balm.'" She handed it to Rod. "Why don't you take this?"

"Really?" Rod took the tube. "Thanks!"

"Sure," Dominique said. "It will make your lips really soft. My boyfriend loves the stuff."

"Is he a model, too?" Mary-Kate asked.

Dominique laughed. "No, he's just a nice guy. Looks aren't everything, you know."

Sylvie shook her head. "Madame La Rouge always says, 'It is all about how you look.' If you ask me, looks *are* everything."

Someone knocked on the dressing-room door. "Five minutes to showtime!"

Sylvie smoothed some bright red lipstick onto Dominique's lips. "Good luck, mademoiselle," she called. Then she packed up her cosmetics brushes and left.

Ashley smiled. Now that Sylvie was gone, she could get down to business. "Tell us more about the other models,

Dominique. How exactly were they acting strange?"

Dominique checked her watch. "Oh, no! I'm sorry, but can we talk about this later? I've got to get onstage."

"Good luck!" Mary-Kate called as she headed for the door.

"And don't worry. We'll be on the lookout," Ashley added. She just wished she knew what she was looking for.

A few minutes later Mary-Kate, Ashley, Rod, and Quincy settled into their seats in the audience.

Ashley read from her computer fact sheet. "Mary-Kate, there are over forty fashion shows scheduled in New York City this week!" she reported. "That means hundreds of models are in town."

"There are tons of celebrities here, too," Mary-Kate added.

"Check it out! There's Madame La Rouge." Mary-Kate pointed to a woman wearing a long, flowing cape.

"Wait till she finds out that Dominique doesn't like to wear cosmetics," Ashley said. "I bet she'll be upset."

Music blasted over the sound system as the fashion show began.

Dominique appeared in a pretty orange-colored dress. She strolled to the end of the stage and smiled.

Mary-Kate and Rod clapped and

cheered, but Ashley was watching Dominique's face. As she stared, she saw one of Dominique's eyebrows begin to twitch. Dominique smiled weakly at the audience and turned to head back. Then she stopped again. Suddenly her feet flew up in a crazy tap dance.

"Is that part of the show?" Mary-Kate asked.

"I don't know," Ashley said.

Dominique cartwheeled down the catwalk. Then she back-flipped right off the stage!

The audience gasped. Dominique's cheeks flushed with embarrassment. She ran backstage.

"Now, *that* was weird," Mary-Kate said.

Ashley nodded. "Well, Special Agent Misty," she said to her sister, "I think we finally know what our assignment is. Dominique said the models were acting strangely. I guess this was what she meant."

"Right." Mary-Kate nodded. "Now we have to find out why!"

Mary-Kate, Ashley, Rod, and Quincy hurried back to the dressing room. They heard voices and stopped in the doorway.

"Just sign this contract," a woman said.

The girls peeked into the dressing room. Dominique sat at her table. She seemed tired and upset.

Renee La Rouge stood beside her, holding a sheet of paper. "Sign here," she said. "And you will be in all of my commercials."

Dominique rubbed her head. "I don't think I want to . . ."

Renee pulled a red lipstick from her purse. She ran the lipstick over Dominique's lips, then put it back in her pocket. "Please, Dominique. I really want to work with you. Sign the contract."

Dominique's eyes glazed over. "Yes, of course," she said. "I would love to sell your cosmetics."

Madame La Rouge placed a pen in Dominique's hand.

"What's going on?" Ashley whispered to Mary-Kate. "Dominique just said she didn't want to work for Renee La Rouge. Now all of a sudden she does."

"Let's go in there," Mary-Kate whispered back. The two girls stepped into the room, followed by Rod and Quincy.

"Hi, Dominique. What's up?" Ashley asked.

"Hi, Madame La Rouge," Mary-Kate said.

Madame La Rouge looked startled. "I'll be back." She grabbed the contract and hurried out of the room.

That's strange, Ashley thought. Why was Renee La Rouge so nervous all of a sudden? Is she hiding something?

Quincy jumped into Dominique's lap. He licked her face—and took off all of her cosmetics with his slobbery tongue.

"D-down, boy," the model sputtered.

"Dominique, is everything all right?" Mary-Kate asked.

"I think so," Dominique said. "I—I just feel a little weird. . . ."

"What happened out on the runway?" Rod asked.

"I—I don't know," Dominique told him. "I didn't want to do that stupid dance and those flips. But I couldn't stop myself. Some of the other models did the same thing last week. Now it's happening to me!"

"And Renee La Rouge asked you to work for her," Mary-Kate added.

Dominique nodded. "I almost agreed. "But . . . I don't really want to work for her."

"So why did you say yes?" Rod asked.

"I don't know," Dominique said. She put her head in her hands. "What's wrong with me?"

Rod stepped close to her. "Don't worry, Dominique," he said. "We'll get to the bottom of this."

"And I know someone who can help us figure it out," Mary-Kate said.

She flipped open her special-agent's bracelet. She punched the "phone" button.

"Hello?" a voice came over the

bracelet's tiny speaker. "What's happening, special agents?"

"IQ, we're headed back to the jet," Mary-Kate said into the bracelet. "We'll need any information you have on Renee La Rouge. And we'll need it right away!"

Mary-Kate, Ashley, Rod, and Quincy raced onboard their private jet. Inside, they found Ivan Quintero sitting in front of his computer.

Mary-Kate and Ashley called Ivan "IQ"

for short. IQ invented all of the cool
gadgets that helped them on their
missions. He made their special bracelets.
He even built Quincy!

"What do you have on Renee La Rouge,
IQ?" Ashley asked.

"I pulled up some stuff on the computer,"
IQ reported. He pressed a few keys
and Renee La Rouge's face appeared on
his monitor.

"Renee is the head of Blush Cosmetics,"

IQ told them. "And she creates all of Blush's cosmetics herself. She's an expert in chemistry."

"According to this report, Blush is one of the most popular brands of cosmetics in the world," Ashley said.

"There's nothing suspicious about that," Quincy pointed out. "Has she ever committed a crime?"

"Good question, Quincy," Mary-Kate said. She patted his head. Quincy rolled over for a belly rub.

"I couldn't find any jail record," IQ replied. "But I'll keep looking." He began to print out his file.

"I still don't get it," Rod said. "Why do you think Renee La Rouge is involved?" He reached into his pocket and took out some lip balm. He unscrewed the cap and rolled it over his lips.

"Renee left in a hurry when we entered

Dominique's dressing room," Ashley reminded him. "That seemed kind of strange, didn't it?"

"But how could Renee make the models do crazy things?" Rod asked. "It doesn't make sense." One of Rod's eyebrows began to twitch. Then he started to giggle.

"What's so funny?" Mary-Kate asked.

"I . . . don't . . . know . . ." Rod was laughing so hard, he could barely speak.

"Come on, Rod. You're totally cracking up," Ashley said. "Tell us the joke."

"There's no joke . . . really!" Rod said through gasps of laughter. "Can't . . . stop. Help! Please!"

"It's like what happened with Dominique," Mary-Kate said. "He's out of control."

"But why?" Ashley asked. "He was just talking to us. Then he put something on his lips. . . ."

"Yeah," Rod said, still laughing. "The lip balm . . . Dominique gave—"

Ashley glanced at her sister. "The new Blush Cosmetics!"

"From Renee's gift basket!" Mary-Kate cried.

IQ held out his hand. "Let's see it."

Rod gave IQ the lip balm. IQ opened the cap and held the tube up to the light. "It looks like regular lip balm to me," he said. "But I'll check it out."

"What should Rod do until then?" Quincy asked.

IQ handed Rod a tissue. "Here," he said. "Take off as much of the stuff as you can. It could be dangerous."

Rod wiped his lips with the tissue. His laughter died down a little. "That's"—he giggled—"a little better."

Ashley glanced out the window. Another private jet was parked next to them on the runway. It was a large pink plane. "Blush Cosmetics" was written

across the side in red letters. It slowly rolled by, getting ready to take off.

"Hey—that's Renee's plane!" Ashley exclaimed. She could see Renee and Sylvie through the window. Renee was punching keys on a tiny red computer.

"She's up to something," Mary-Kate said.

"And we've got to find out what it is," Ashley agreed. "Fire up the jet, Mary-Kate. And follow that plane!"

"Paris is so beautiful!" Mary-Kate exclaimed. She flew the jet over the city. They zoomed past the Eiffel Tower.

"*Magnifique!*" Ashley agreed. She peered down at her book, a pocket guide to France. "Did you know that Paris is the home to some of the most amazing fashions in the world?"

Mary-Kate chuckled. "Forget it, Ashley. We're not here to go shopping."

"I know." Ashley sighed. "What a waste."

Rod listened to his headset. "We're cleared . . . for landing." He giggled.

Ashley glanced at him. "I hope the Blush lip balm wears off soon."

"Me . . . too!" Rod snickered.

Mary-Kate landed the jet on a private airstrip. Then the two girls, Rod, and Quincy hopped into a waiting car. Rod drove them into the city.

"Let's snoop around Renee's

headquarters," Mary-Kate said. "I'll bet that's where she's headed."

"Wait—let's stop at a department store first," Ashley said. "I want to see if anything strange is going on at the Blush cosmetics counter."

"Good idea," Mary-Kate agreed.

Rod pulled up to a big department store. Mary-Kate and Ashley ran inside.

Mary-Kate searched the Blush Cosmetics counter for the line of Face Values cosmetics. But she didn't see it anywhere.

"May I help you?" a saleswoman asked.

"Yes," Mary-Kate replied. "We were wondering if you sell Face Values cosmetics."

"I will have it in a few days," the woman said. "Madame La Rouge says the products are fantastic! My sister is a model. Since she tried Face Values, she can't stop smiling!"

Ashley thought about Rod's laughing. "Yes, her products seem to have that effect on people," she said.

The woman smiled at the girls. "Come back next week. We're giving away free samples of Face Values with every purchase."

"Thanks. Maybe we will," Ashley told the saleswoman. The girls walked away.

"Time to find Madame La Rouge," Mary-Kate said. She opened her special-agent bracelet. "Paris. Ten A.M. Now heading to Blush Cosmetics."

They passed through the video department on their way back to the car. The area was filled with huge televisions. The news was playing on every screen.

"The fashion world was shocked today when teen supermodel Dominique ran off the runway," a female reporter said.

Ashley and Mary-Kate stopped to listen.

"She did a strange dance and . . . and . . ." The reporter's eyebrow began to twitch.

"Wait a minute!" Ashley cried. "I've seen that twitch before!"

"Yes! We saw it on Dominique and Rod," Mary-Kate agreed.

"I'm sorry," the reporter said. "I've got something in my eye." She took a bright red cosmetics case off her desk. She opened it to check her eye.

Ashley gasped. She had seen that red

case before. "Oh, no!" she cried. "That reporter is using Face Values cosmetics!"

"Where was I?" the reporter said. "Oh, yes—speaking of fashion, I can't say enough about Blush Cosmetics. Renee La Rouge has a new line of cosmetics called Face Values. Go buy it. Trust me, it will change your life."

The reporter shivered. She glanced around, confused. "What did I just say? Where am I?" she asked.

"It's so weird," Ashley said. "Everyone who uses Face Values cosmetics ends up doing something they don't want to."

"Renee's behind this." Mary-Kate frowned. "And next week she's giving away tons of Face Values samples. Who knows what people will be forced to do then?"

Ashley gasped. "Come on. We've got to stop Renee before it's too late!"

CHAPTER FOUR
A Sneaky Surprise

"This is it," Rod said, still laughing. The car stopped in front of a fancy red building. "Blush Cosmetics."

Ashley, Mary-Kate, and Quincy jumped out of the car and hurried into the building. A tall statue of Renee La Rouge stood in the middle of a big, fancy lobby.

"Eleven A.M. Blush headquarters. For some reason, this place gives me the creeps!" Mary-Kate said into her bracelet.

Quincy sniffed at the lobby's marble floor. "Grrrrrr."

"What is it, Quincy?" Ashley whispered.

Quincy stopped sniffing. "I smell someone coming."

"Quick, hide!" Mary-Kate whispered.

Mary-Kate, Ashley, and Quincy ducked behind the statue of Renee La Rouge. Sylvie, the cosmetics artist, glided into the lobby. Then she slipped through a doorway and disappeared.

"Let's follow her," Ashley said. "She might lead us to Renee."

Mary-Kate, Ashley, and Quincy ran across the lobby and slipped through the doorway. They found themselves in a long hallway lined with more doors. Sylvie was nowhere to be seen.

"Where did she go?" Ashley asked.

Mary-Kate opened the first door she came to. "Look!" she whispered. "A lab!"

The lab was filled with bubbling beakers and tubes. "This must be where Renee makes her cosmetics," Ashley said. She grabbed a red bottle marked "Face Values."

"I wonder what could be in this stuff?" Mary-Kate said.

"Wouldn't you like to know." A woman spoke up behind them.

The girls whirled around. There, in the doorway, stood Sylvie and Renee La Rouge!

"It's those girls from New York," Sylvie said. "Misty and Amber. Dominique's friends!"

"Friends?" Renee scowled. "They look more like spies if you ask me."

Quincy barked at the women.

"We know you're up to something,

Renee," Mary-Kate said. "But you'll never get away with it."

"We'll see about that," Renee warned. "I've got big plans, and no one is going to stop me. I'm afraid I'll have to get rid of the two of you—and your little dog—in my own special way."

"I still think we should handcuff them to the chairs, Madame," Sylvie said. "It would be more secure."

"Handcuffs?" Renee snapped. "*Please.* Handcuffs would look terrible! And what's my motto, Sylvie?"

"'It's all about how you look,'" Sylvie said.

Quincy growled and barked. Renee grabbed him and stuffed him into a cage. She slammed the wire door shut and locked it.

"What are you going to do with us?" Ashley asked.

"What I do best," Renee replied. "Give you a makeover."

Ashley glanced at her sister, worried. She knew Renee would use Face Values cosmetics. What would happen to them?

Sylvie headed for the door. "I need to check on production, Madame. Will you be all right here on your own?"

"Of course," Renee replied. "When you get back, Misty and Amber will do whatever I say."

Mary-Kate squirmed in her chair. "What makes you so sure?" she asked. "Do the cosmetics help you control people's minds or something?"

Renee La Rouge smiled slowly.

Ashley gasped. It was true! "So *that's* how you get people to do things they don't want to do," she said. "That's how you controlled Dominique!"

"Very smart, girls," Renee told them. "Too smart."

She dipped her cosmetics brush into some Face Values powder and leaned close to Mary-Kate. Mary-Kate turned her head away.

"Stay still!" Renee shouted. She twisted Mary-Kate's face toward her and swept the brush over it.

"Accept it, girls," Renee said sweetly. "Face Values will change not only you, but the whole world!"

She brushed powder onto Ashley's face, too. "Everyone wearing my products will be completely in my power!"

Renee twisted open a tube of red lipstick. She gripped Mary-Kate's chin hard. Then she spread lipstick across Mary-Kate's mouth.

"Lots of women buy your products," Mary-Kate said. "But what about all the men in the world? They don't wear your cosmetics."

Renee turned and painted Ashley's lips.

"Ah, that is the genius of my plan. Soon women all over the world will buy Face Values. And each of them will receive a free gift—lip balm and men's cologne. They will give these gifts to the men in their lives. Once I get them hooked—"

"You'll control the world!" Ashley exclaimed. She shivered. Renee's plan could actually work!

"Then I will make people dress with style again! And, of course, I will have them buy all of my products. I will be the richest woman in the world!" Renee smiled. "What more could a girl want?"

"Why are you so worried about how people look, anyway?" Mary-Kate asked.

"Yeah," Ashley said. "After all, it's what's on the inside that matters, right?"

Renee sighed. "What nonsense. It's all about how you look on the *outside*." She paused to dot a little more powder

on Mary-Kate's nose. "Well, your makeover is done. And now for the finishing touch."

She removed a little red computer from her pocket. It was the same computer Ashley had seen her using on her jet— right before Rod started laughing!

"Excuse me, Madame," Sylvie burst into the room. "They need you in the packaging room right away!"

Renee slipped the computer back into her pocket. "Just relax and make yourselves comfortable, girls. Soon you will be completely in my power!"

CHAPTER SIX
The Last Laugh

Renee grabbed Quincy and left the lab. Sylvie followed her out.

Ashley glanced at Mary-Kate. "I don't feel any different. Do you?"

"Nope." Mary-Kate shook her head.

"Excellent!" Ashley said. "Those special facial masks IQ made protected us from Renee's cosmetics!"

"Thank goodness," Mary-Kate said. "I just have one question. What kind of evil genius ties up her enemies with a big red bow?" She tugged on the ribbon.

Ashley shrugged. "One who likes things pretty, I guess."

The girls wiggled in their chairs. Soon the silky ribbons came loose. They jumped to their feet.

Ashley and Mary-Kate peeled off their facial masks. All the cosmetics Renee had applied came off with the masks. They threw the gooey mess into a trash can by the door.

"Phew!" Ashley said. "That feels better!"

Mary-Kate nodded. "Let's go save the world . . . again!"

"You know it, sister," Ashley answered.

"Solid!" Mary-Kate said. "Now let's find Renee by tracking Quincy's radar signal."

Ashley flipped open her special-agent bracelet. It beeped. "Quincy's location is locked in," she said. "Let's move!"

Ashley and Mary-Kate peeked through an open doorway down the hall from the lab. Inside, Ashley found a large room filled with hundreds of workers in pink

jumpsuits. They were putting together Face Values gift packages! Renee and Sylvie watched over the workers.

"Twelve P.M. Blush headquarters," Mary-Kate whispered into her special-agent bracelet. "Special Agent Amber and I must foil Renee's plan to—"

"Will you stop doing that!" Ashley interrupted. "We don't want Renee to hear us!"

"Sorry," Mary-Kate said.

"Everything is in order here," Renee announced. "We'll ship Face Values to the stores tomorrow. Soon I will control minds all over the world!"

"Yes, Madame," Sylvie said. "Congratulations."

Ashley spotted Quincy. "He's over there!" she whispered to Mary-Kate. "Renee's got him."

Renee pulled the little red computer from her pocket. "Oh, Sylvie . . ." she called.

"Yes, Madame?" Sylvie answered.

Renee punched some buttons on the computer. Sylvie threw her head back. She started laughing and laughing.

"Oh, I love it!" Renee cried. "This is going to be so much fun!"

Sylvie is laughing for no reason, Ashley realized. Just like Rod was laughing after he used the Face Values lip balm.

"Check it out, Mary-Kate," Ashley said. "Renee controls people who wear Face Values. But she needs that little computer to do it!"

Mary-Kate frowned. "Let's go stop her."

Mary-Kate and Ashley stepped out of the shadows. "Not so fast, Renee," Mary-Kate called.

"You're too late," Renee cried. "Besides,

you're already under my control." She
pressed a button on the tiny computer.

"No, we're not!" Ashley cried. "Your
cosmetics didn't work on us." She turned
to Mary-Kate. "Quick! Let's grab Renee's
computer!"

Mary-Kate rushed toward Renee La
Rouge.

"You'll never get it!" Renee cried. She
tossed the tiny computer to Sylvie.

Ashley tried to
grab it from Sylvie—
too late.

Still laughing, Sylvie threw the computer back to Renee.

"Mary-Kate! Get her!" Ashley cried.

As the computer sailed through the air, Mary-Kate darted across the room. *Wham!* She tackled Renee to the ground.

The computer hit the floor with a loud crack. It broke into tiny pieces.

Sylvie suddenly stopped laughing, and Ashley knew it was all over. The computer was trashed. Without it, Renee couldn't control anybody.

Renee fell to her knees. "Noooo! My life's work! It's ruined!" She moaned. "I'll get you—if it's the last thing I do!"

"Yeah, right," Mary-Kate said. Quincy jumped up into her arms.

"I don't think so," Ashley added. She flipped open her special-agent bracelet. She hit the phone button. "IQ, get Headquarters on the line. Tell them we just short-circuited another evil plan!"

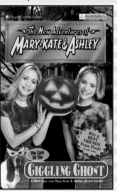

mary-kateandashley
awholenewlook

MARY-KATE AND ASHLEY in ACTION!

look for other books in this
brand-new book series

**LOOK FOR
MARY-KATE AND ASHLEY in ACTION! #3
FUBBLE BUBBLE TROUBLE
COMING SOON!**

GAMES

BOOKS

FASHION
DOLLS

CALENDARS

mary-kateandashley.com
America Online Keyword: mary-kateandashley

mary-kateandashley

DVDs AND VIDEOS

mary-kateandashley
let us entertain you

CDs

DUALSTAR
CONSUMER PRODUCTS

Let's go save
the world . . . again!

MARY-KATE AND ASHLEY
iN ACTION!

Book #2
The Dream Team

URGENT MESSAGE

FROM: Headquarters

TO: Special Agents Misty and Amber

LOCATION: Rome, Italy. The Global Games.

PROBLEM: The Hipslovian gymnastics team is good—too good. Their flips, jumps, and vaults seem super-human. We know that team captain, Grudmilla, will stop at nothing to win the gold.

YOUR MISSION: Disguise yourselves as gymnasts, fly to Rome, and find out if the Hipslovian gymnasts are really a perfect ten—or perfect cheaters.

ENTER BELOW FOR YOUR CHANCE TO WIN A FRAMED, AUTOGRAPHED

MARY-KATE AND ASHLEY
in ACTION!

ANIMATED IMAGE!*

*Prize may differ from image shown above

MARY-KATE AND ASHLEY in ACTION!
Win Cool Mary-Kate and Ashley in ACTION! Prizes Sweepstakes

OFFICIAL RULES:

1. No purchase necessary.

2. To enter complete the official entry form or hand print your name, address, age, and phone number along with the words "Win Cool *Mary-Kate and Ashley in ACTION!* Prizes Sweepstakes" on a 3" x 5" card and mail to: Win Cool *Mary-Kate and Ashley in ACTION!* Prizes Sweepstakes, c/o HarperEntertainment, Attn: Children's Marketing Department, 10 East 53rd Street, New York, NY 10022. Entries must be received by January 31, 2003. Enter as often as you wish, but each entry must be mailed separately. One entry per envelope. Partially completed, illegible, or mechanically reproduced entries will not be accepted. Sponsors are not responsible for lost, late, mutilated, illegible, stolen, postage due, incomplete, or misdirected entries. All entries become the property of Dualstar Entertainment Group, LLC, and will not be returned.

3. Sweepstakes open to all legal residents of the United States, (excluding Colorado and Rhode Island), who are between the ages of five and fifteen on January 31, 2003, excluding employees and immediate family members of HarperCollins Publishers, Inc. ("HarperCollins"), Parachute Properties and Parachute Press, Inc., and their respective subsidiaries and affiliates, officers, directors, shareholders, employees, agents, attorneys, and other representatives (individually and collectively "Parachute"), Dualstar Entertainment Group, LLC, and its subsidiaries and affiliates, officers, directors, shareholders, employees, agents, attorneys, and other representatives (individually and collectively "Dualstar"), and their respective parent companies, affiliates, subsidiaries, advertising, promotion and fulfillment agencies, and the persons with whom each of the above are domiciled. Offer void where prohibited or restricted by law.

4. Odds of winning depend on the total number of entries received. Approximately 225,000 sweepstakes announcements published. All prizes will be awarded. Winner will be randomly drawn on or about February 15, 2003, by HarperEntertainment, whose decisions are final. Potential winner will be notified by mail and will be required to sign and return an affidavit of eligibility and release of liability within 14 days of notification. Prize won by minors will be awarded to parent or legal guardian who must sign and return all required legal documents. By acceptance of his or her prize, winner consents to the use of his or her name, photograph, likeness, and personal information by HarperCollins, Parachute, Dualstar, and for publicity purposes without further compensation except where prohibited.

5. a) One (1) Grand Prize Winner will win three images from an episode of *Mary-Kate and Ashley in ACTION!* in one frame, with Mary-Kate and Ashley's autograph. Sponsor to select images. HarperCollins, Parachute, and Dualstar reserve the right to substitute another prize of equal or of greater value in the event that the winner is unable to receive the prize for any reason. Approximate retail value: $665.00.

   b) Twenty-five (25) First Prize Winners will win a custom *Mary-Kate and Ashley in ACTION!* sweatshirt. Approximate retail value: $22.00 each.

6. Only one prize will be awarded per individual, family, or household. Prizes are non-transferable and cannot be sold or redeemed for cash. No cash substitute is available. Any federal, state, or local taxes are the responsibility of the winner. Sponsor may substitute prize of equal or greater value, if necessary, due to availability.

7. Additional terms: By participating, entrants agree a) to the official rules and decisions of the judges, which will be final in all respects; and b) to waive any claim to ambiguity of the official rules and b) to release, discharge, and hold harmless HarperCollins, Parachute, Dualstar, and their affiliates, subsidiaries, and advertising and promotion agencies from and against any and all liability or damages associated with acceptance, use, or misuse of any prize received in this sweepstakes.

8. Any dispute arising from this Sweepstakes will be determined according to the laws of the State of New York, without reference to its conflict of law principles, and the entrants consent to the personal jurisdiction of the State and Federal courts located in New York County and agree that such courts have exclusive jurisdiction over all such disputes.

9. To obtain the name of the winner, please send your request and a self-addressed stamped envelope (excluding residents of Vermont and Washington) to Win Cool *Mary-Kate and Ashley in ACTION!* Prizes Sweepstakes, c/o HarperEntertainment, Attn: Children's Marketing Department, 10 East 53rd Street, New York, NY 10022 by March 1, 2003. Sweepstakes Sponsor: HarperCollins Publishers, Inc.